Tiny Baby Jesus

written by

Dandi Daley Mackall

illustrated by

Julia Noonan

ZONDER**kidz**

ZONDERVAN.com/
AUTHORTRACKER
follow your favorite authors

To "Ellie," Helen Isabella Hendren, my first granddaughter!

Jesus was a baby too.

D.M.

In memory of my godfather, James Richardson.

With special thanks to the Dellomo family, and Matt, and Jo.

J.N.

ZONDERKIDZ

Tiny Baby Jesus
Copyright © 2009 by Dandi Daley Mackall
Illustrations copyright © 2009 by Julia Noonan

Requests for information should be addressed to:
Zonderkidz, *Grand Rapids, Michigan 49530*

Library of Congress Cataloging-in-Publication Data

Mackall, Dandi Daley.
    Tiny Baby Jesus / by Dandi Daley Mackall
    p. cm.
    ISBN 978-0-310-71799-7 (hardcover)
        [1. Jesus Christ—Nativity—Juvenile literature.   2. Jesus Christ—Biography—
    Juvenile literature.] I. Title.
    BT315.3.M33 2009
    232.9'01—dc22
    {B}
                                                                2008038671

Editor: Betsy Flikkema
Art direction & design: Kris Nelson

Printed in China

10 11 12 13 • 5 4 3 2

Since the children have flesh and blood, he [Jesus] too shared in their humanity.

Hebrews 2:14

Tiny, tiny fingers touch a piece of hay.
Tiny baby Jesus born in Bethlehem today.

Now those very fingers,
grown so sure and strong—
Jesus is a carpenter,
working all day long.

Tiny feet of Jesus,
kicking up a storm.
Angels circling round his bed
keep him safe and warm.

Now those feet are bigger,
walking on the sea,
leaving us his footsteps,
saying, "Come and follow me!"

Tiny baby shoulders
wrapped in swaddling clothes.
Joseph stands by Mary's side,
knowing what he knows.

Now the lame and lepers
find their victory,
leaning on the shoulders
of the man from Galilee.

Tiny mouth of Jesus,
soft and sweet and mild.
Shepherds stare in wonder
at the promised holy child.

From the mouth of Jesus words flow night and day,
sharing love through stories and teaching how to pray.

Tiny baby Jesus, eyes so clear and bright.
Wise men seek the newborn King on this starry night.

Tender eyes of Jesus see the needs of man.
Jesus offers peace on earth as only Jesus can.

Tiny baby Jesus, precious little arms.
Mary bends to kiss your cheek,
pondering your charms.

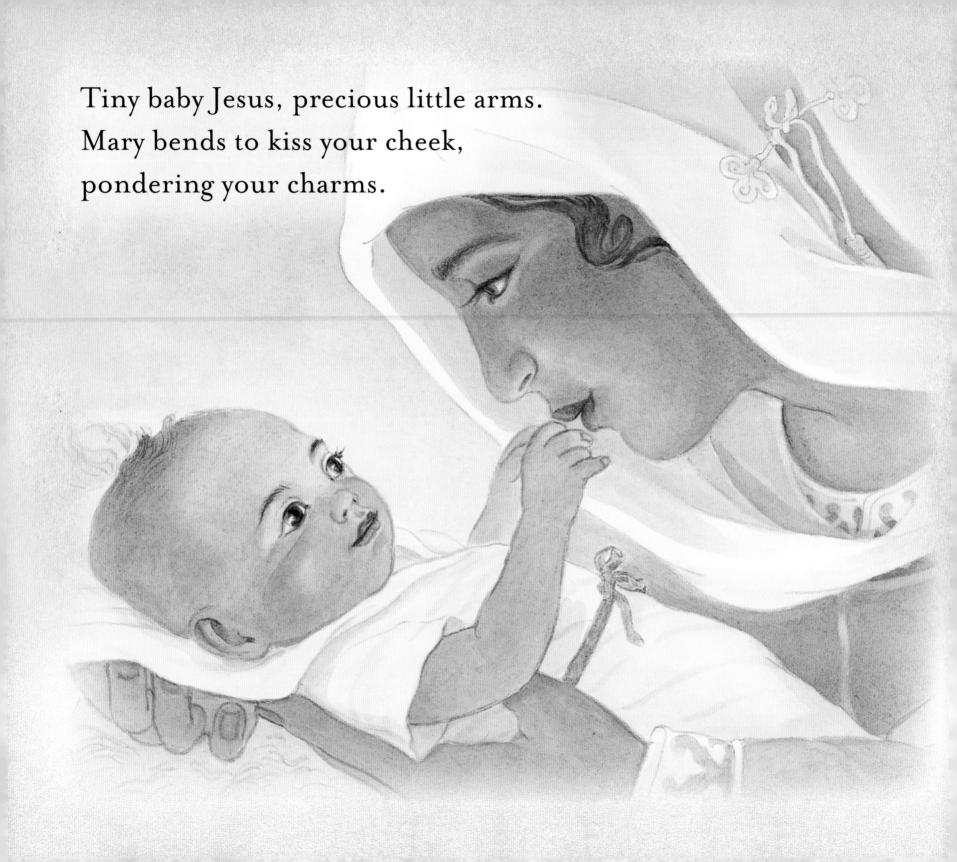

Seated with disciples,
one last time to dine.
Arms of Jesus reaching out
pass the bread and wine.

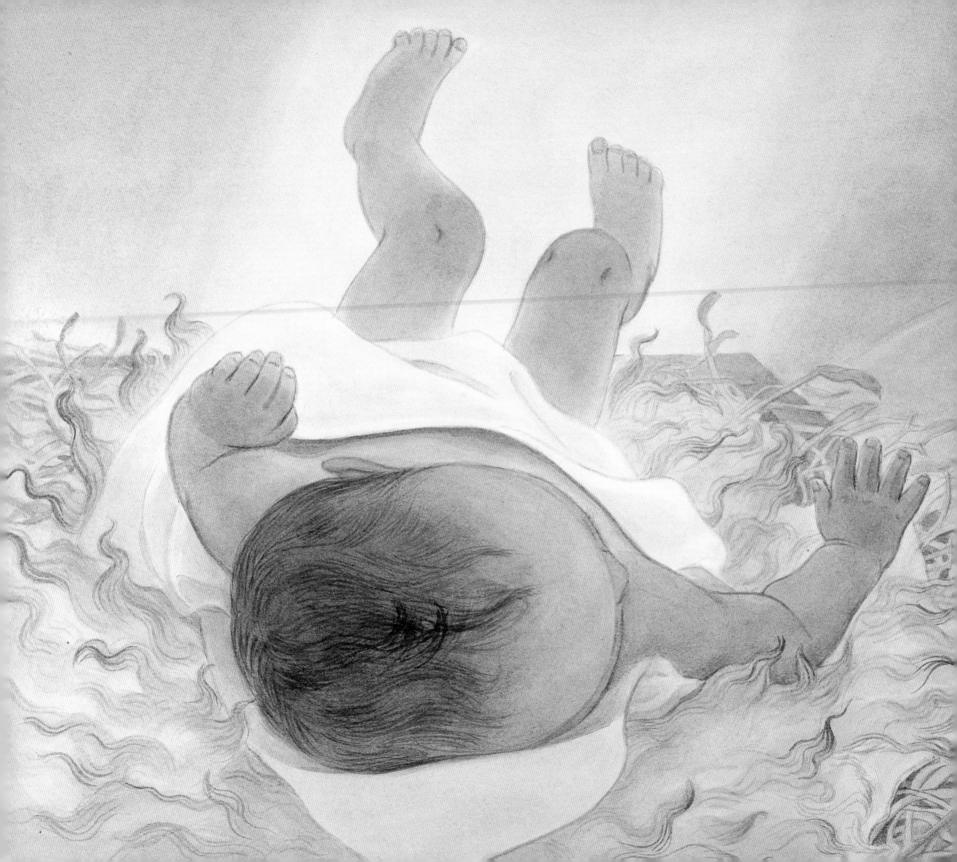

Tiny baby Jesus,
wrinkly, knobby knees.
Hovering cows and donkeys
shield you from the breeze.

Jesus in the garden kneels alone to pray.
Bowed before his Father, willing to obey.

Tiny baby Jesus,
beating human heart.
Those around you
sense your love
from the very start.

Heart as big as heaven—Savior is your name.
Jesus died and rose again—that's why Jesus came.

Tiny gift from heaven,
sent to us on earth.
God's Son wrapped for Christmas
in a miracle of birth.